D1712243

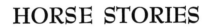

HORSE STORIES

The
Basic Vocabulary Series

The books in the *Basic Vocabulary Series* are written with charm of style and high interest appeal for the children. Children love to read them for fun and thus get a vast amount of practice in reading skills. A high literary quality has been maintained in writing these true stories of animals, and retelling tales of folklore.

These Basic Vocabulary books are written with the Dolch 220 Basic Sight Words. The words make up two-thirds or more of all primary reading books and more than half of all other school books. The Dolch 95 Commonest Nouns have also been used. In addition to words from these two basic lists, each book has an average of about one new word per page.

This Series is prepared under the direction of Edward W. Dolch, Ph.D., Professor of Education, Emeritus, University of Illinois. The books in this series are:

Animal Stories	Lion and Tiger Stories
Bear Stories	Lodge Stories
Circus Stories	More Dog Stories
Dog Stories	Navaho Stories
Elephant Stories	Pueblo Stories
Folk Stories	Tepee Stories
Horse Stories	"Why" Stories
Irish Stories	Wigwam Stories

HORSE STORIES
IN BASIC VOCABULARY

By

EDWARD W. DOLCH

and

MARGUERITE P. DOLCH

Illustrated by

CHARLES FORSYTHE

GARRARD PUBLISHING COMPANY
CHAMPAIGN, ILLINOIS

Foreword

In all times, man's best friend—next to his dog—has been his horse. Horses have worked for men, both in the country and on the streets of the city. Horses have gone into battle with their masters. And horses have taken part in many kinds of hunting all over the world. Even though machines have often taken the place of the horse at work, men still like to ride horseback, men still watch horseraces, and men still have horses as their pets and friends.

In this book are true stories of things that horses have actually been seen to do. Men who have lived with horses have told these stories. Some of these horses have been in the circus. Some have been simple work horses. Some have been race horses. Some have lived on western cow ranches. The stories are often remarkable—for horses have done remarkable things. Horses have intelligence; they have love and affection. And these men have had love and affection for horses.

There is a great library of horse stories. It is hoped that after reading this book, the reader will go to some of these other interesting books and come to know more of our friend—the horse.

Urbana, Ill.

E. W. Dolch

List of Pictures

Contents

A Smart Cow Pony

A cowboy needs a good cow pony. But not every horse makes a good cow pony.

A cow pony is not a very big horse. He is sometimes very wild. When a man tries to ride him, a cow pony sometimes bucks and bucks. That is, he tries to throw the man off his back. It takes a man who knows about horses to teach a cow pony to let a man ride him.

Brown Jug was a very smart cow pony. At first he did not want anyone to ride upon his back. But he had a good cowboy to teach him. At first, the cowboy talked to the horse just as if the horse were another man. He told the cow pony that a good horse had to learn to work. He had to learn to work with a man on his back.

Brown Jug stood still. He even let the friendly man put a saddle on his back. But when the man got into the saddle, oh, how Brown Jug bucked. He bucked and bucked and bucked. But the man stayed on his back.

Day after day, that man came and put the saddle on Brown

Jug's back. He always talked to the horse in a friendly way. But as soon as the man got into the saddle, Brown Jug bucked. But the man still stayed on his back.

But one day, as soon as the saddle was on, Brown Jug started to buck.

The man pulled on the rope that was on the horse's head in a way that threw Brown Jug to the ground. And before Brown Jug knew what had happened, the cowboy had tied Brown Jug's feet together.

Then the cowboy sat right on Brown Jug and talked to him.

He talked to him a long, long time. At last the cowboy let Brown Jug get up.

That day Brown Jug let the cowboy ride him without bucking. The little horse tried to do what the man wanted him to do.

That day Brown Jug began to learn to be a good cow pony. But always, when the cowboy got on Brown Jug, he had to buck a little just to show what he could do. And then he went about his work.

Now the work of a cow pony is very hard. He has to learn to make the cows go the way the cowboy wants them to go. And many times the cows want to go just the way they want to go.

Then too, the cow pony has to learn to get just one cow away from the other cows and to make it go through a gate. The cowboy tells the cow pony which cow he wants. The cow pony understands. He goes right in among the cows and gets that one cow away from the other cows. That is called "cutting out" a cow.

Brown Jug became a very good cow pony. One day he showed what a smart horse he was.

The cowboy and Brown Jug were "cutting out" a great big cow from the other cows. This big cow was angry and she did not want to go the way the cowboy wanted her to go.

The big cow would go the way she herself wanted to go. And Brown Jug would head her off. Then the big cow would run back to the other cows.

A cow pony has to run very fast and stop suddenly, then turn and run very fast the other way.

All at once, Brown Jug stepped into a hole in the ground. Over he went. And the cowboy was thrown off his back.

But Brown Jug knew that he had to get that big cow away from the other cows. He got to his feet. He did not need a cowboy to tell him what to do. He went after that cow all by himself. He got that cow away from the other cows. He made that cow go through the gate.

And how that cowboy laughed. He patted Brown Jug and said,

"If there were more cow ponies like you, Brown Jug, we would not need to have cowboys."

Joe, the Cowboy

Joe was a young man who could ride a horse as well as any cowboy. He had been asked by a friend to help drive a herd of wild horses.

"Come on over," said Mr. Henry. "And I will give you a good horse to ride. We have the herd of wild horses rounded up. We need all the help we can get."

"That is just what I would like to do," said Joe. And so Joe went with Mr. Henry.

The next morning, the cowboys

went out to the corral to catch their horses.

Mr. Henry showed Joe a horse at the far side of the corral.

"There is your horse, Joe," said Mr. Henry. "He is not as young as he used to be. But you will never ride a better horse."

Joe did not know what to think when he looked at the horse. He had never seen such a horse. The other horses were running around the corral. The cowboys were having a hard time catching them. But Joe's horse just stood still. He let Joe walk right up to him. He let Joe put the saddle on his back. And then the horse stood still with his head hanging down almost to the ground. Joe's horse looked as if he did not care about anything.

When Joe got on his horse, he found that it was a very good riding horse. He followed Mr. Henry and the cowboys out to where the herd of wild horses was kept.

And now began the long drive over the grass country. The horses went slowly, eating the grass along the way. The cowboys kept watch. They did not want the horses to become frightened.

Day after day, the cowboys rode slowly along. The country changed. The grass country became country that was covered with brush and small trees. A road had been made through the brush. It was very hot.

Joe and two cowboys were riding down this road among the horses. Suddenly ahead of them, they heard a noise. The horses heard the noise too. They lifted their heads. The wild horses right ahead of Joe became frightened.

The frightened horses left the road and rushed into the brush.

"We will have to get those horses back to the road before all the horses become frightened," called one of the cowboys."

The cowboys rode right into the brush after the frightened horses.

Joe could not see how a horse could get through that brush. He did not know what to do. But Joe's horse knew what to do. He went into the brush right after the cowboys. It was all Joe could do to stay on his horse.

Joe's horse knew that he must

get the frightened horses back to the road. He got through the brush somehow. Sometimes he backed through the brush. Sometimes he gave little jumps to make his way through. The brush hurt Joe, and the brush hurt the horse. They were both scratched and bleeding.

The first thing that Joe knew was that he had left the cowboys behind. His horse got through the brush and out into an open place. Wild horses were all around Joe. He was sure that he was going to be killed. But Joe's horse knew what to do.

Joe's horse ran ahead of the wild horses. He made the first horse turn around. As the first horse turned, the wild horses following him ran into him. The wild horses were all around Joe and his horse.

Then Joe heard the cowboys coming. They had come out of the brush into the open. They knew how to turn the wild horses and get them to go back to the road. And Joe's horse knew just what to do to help.

At last the wild horses were together again. A place was

found beside the road where grass grew. The horses ate the grass and the cowboys rested.

Joe looked at his horse. The horse was scratched and bleeding. He was not a nice-looking horse. But Joe thought he was the most beautiful horse that he had ever seen. As Joe was trying to take care of his bleeding horse, he heard the cowboys talking,

"That new man, Joe, is a good cowboy. And that horse of his is a fast horse. He got to those wild horses before we did and had almost turned them. That new man, Joe, is a good cowboy."

Joe said into his horse's ear,
"You did it all, old boy. I just
went along for the ride."

Old Red

The cowboys down in Texas like to tell about Old Red.

Every year, the cowboys had to ride into the brush. They had to round up the cows and the calves. The calves had to be branded so that everyone would know who owned them.

Every year the cowboys would see a big red steer. But no cowboy could ever get a rope over the long horns of this big red steer. The cowboys called this steer Old Red.

Old Red knew just where to

hide. No cowboy was ever going to rope him and drive him in.

Cowboys could never get the cows and their calves out of the brush without the help of their cow ponies. These cow ponies are small horses. They are very smart horses. They can run very fast. But they can stop suddenly.

When a cowboy going after a cow could get his rope over the cow's horns, the cow pony would suddenly turn and pull back hard. The cow would fall to the ground. The cowboy would jump down, run to the cow, and tie its feet together. All the time, the pony would be pulling on the rope so that the cow could not get up.

The cow that was tied up would be left on the ground over night. In the morning, she would be sure to go along with the herd.

One night, there was a big moon. The cowboys thought they would round up some of the cows in the moonlight. Very quietly, they rode through the brush.

They found some cows eating grass in the moonlight. And with the cows was a big red steer. The cowboys threw their ropes.

They caught many of the cows. And one cowboy got his rope over the horns of the big red steer just as it ran into the brush.

The cow pony stopped suddenly but he did not throw the steer. Each one pulled on the rope. Then the red steer turned in the brush and rushed at the cow pony. The cowboy saw that the steer was Old Red.

But when Old Red turned, he came around a small tree. He rushed at the cow pony, but came to the end of the rope that was around the tree. The sudden stop threw Old Red around so that his back end hit the pony.

The cowboy got hold of the steer's tail, and pulled as hard as he could. And he called for help with all his might.

The other cowboys came riding up. They got their ropes on Old Red. They threw him down. And they tied him to the tree. They would come back for him in the morning.

How the cowboys laughed when they told about Old Red. Old Red, the steer that no cowboy could catch, had been caught by the tail.

Coaly-Bay

Coaly-Bay was a beautiful horse. His body was reddish brown like a bay-colored horse. His legs and tail and mane were coal black. And that was why the horse trainer called him Coaly-Bay.

When Coaly-Bay was three years old, the horse trainer went out to the pasture. It was time for Coaly-Bay to have a saddle on his back. It was time that Coaly-Bay learned to let someone ride him.

The horse trainer got the

saddle on Coaly-Bay's back. But Coaly-Bay did not think as the horse trainer did. He was not going to let any man ride on his back if he could help it. The beautiful horse bucked and bucked and bucked.

The horse trainer knew just how to train a horse. Coaly-Bay bucked and bucked every time a saddle was put on his back, but at last he let the horse trainer ride him.

Coaly-Bay found out that if he bucked and bucked, the man on his back hurt him. And so for a time Coaly-Bay was a good horse. But Coaly-Bay was not going to let every man ride upon his back if he could help it. After a little time, the beautiful horse was lame.

Coaly-Bay could hardly walk. He held up one of his front legs. The horse trainer looked at the leg. He could not see that anything was wrong with the leg. But Coaly-Bay could not walk. He limped and limped.

The horse trainer knew that you could not ride a lame horse. He put Coaly-Bay back into the pasture with the other horses so that his leg would get well.

Coaly-Bay limped over to the other horses. He stood with them, hanging his head as if he were very sick.

In a day or two Coaly-Bay was all right. He was running around the pasture with the other horses. The horse trainer caught him, put the saddle on his back, and rode him. Coaly-Bay did not buck. He let the horse trainer ride upon his back. But poor Coaly-Bay was lame again. And back he went into the pasture.

On one side of the pasture was a high fence. And on the other side of the fence was a neighbor's garden. The neighbor had put up the high fence so that the horses from the pasture could not get into his garden.

But every night some horse got into his garden. The neighbor came to the horse trainer and said, "You must keep your horses out of my garden."

The horse trainer said, "My horses could not get into your garden. They could not jump over that high fence."

The neighbor was very angry and said, "Some horse gets into my garden every night."

The horse trainer said to his

neighbor, "I will stay up with you tonight and watch. We will find out what horse gets into your garden."

That night the horse trainer watched with his neighbor. It was not long before they saw Coaly-Bay jump over the high fence and get into the garden.

Now the horse trainer knew that Coaly-Bay was not a lame horse. No lame horse could jump over such a high fence. He also knew that Coaly-Bay was not a good riding horse.

"It is too bad that my horse has hurt your garden," said the horse trainer. "I cannot keep Coaly-Bay on my side of the high fence. I will give him to you. He is a beautiful horse."

Coaly-Bay went to live with the neighbor. But he would not let the neighbor ride on his back. One day he hurt the neighbor's boy who tried to ride him.

The neighbor was afraid that this bad horse would kill someone.

The neighbor put a sign on his front fence:

HORSE FOR SALE

Bear Hunters

Six men wanted to go into the Bear Country to hunt bears. They had to go far into the mountains. Their things were carried by pack horses. And they had guns and everything they needed to hunt bears. But they had no bear bait.

Sometimes bears are very hard to find. Then hunters take bear bait with them. They take an old horse or an old cow with them into the Bear Country. The hunters kill the old horse or the old cow at a place where the bears can find it.

The six bear hunters saw the sign on the fence:

HORSE FOR SALE

"Maybe we can buy an old horse for 'bear bait,'" said one of the hunters.

When the hunter saw beautiful Coaly-Bay he said, "We do not want to buy a riding horse. We want to buy an old horse for bear bait. Five dollars is all that we will give for an old horse."

The neighbor with the garden wanted to sell Coaly-Bay. And so he said to the hunter, "Give me the five dollars and take the horse. I don't want to keep him."

The hunter gave him the five dollars and then he said, "Now tell me why you would sell such a beautiful horse for five dollars."

"You cannot ride him," said the man. "He can run and jump when he is going the way he wants to go. But when you want him to do something, this horse is lame and sick. He is a bad horse."

"Well," said the hunter, "this horse is beautiful bear bait."

The hunters went far into the mountains. Coaly-Bay was driven ahead with the pack horses. Coaly-Bay was very lame.

But one day when Coaly-Bay saw that the men were not looking, away he ran. He was not lame at all.

One of the men who knew the country, got on his horse and went after Coaly-Bay. He caught up with Coaly-Bay near some big rocks.

When Coaly-Bay saw the man, he turned and went back to the other horses. But he was a very lame horse. He limped so badly that he could hardly walk.

When Coaly-Bay got back with the other horses, he bit one of the pack horses and hurt him. Coaly-Bay was a very bad horse.

The hunters were now in Bear Country. They thought that they had better put out their bear bait. The next morning, two of the hunters drove Coaly-Bay up the mountain. This morning Coaly-Bay was not lame. He held his head high. The wind blew his black mane and his long tail.

"I do not want to shoot such a beautiful horse," said one of the hunters.

"I know," said the other hunter, "but he is a bad horse and we must have bear bait."

The hunter got his gun ready to shoot.

The other hunter whistled so that Coaly-Bay would turn around.

The hunter fired his gun.

But Coaly-Bay did not fall to the ground. He ran away as fast as he could go. The hunter had not hit him.

"I don't do that very often," said the hunter. "The sun must have been in my eyes."

"I am glad you did not kill that beautiful horse," said the other hunter.

Coaly-Bay ran and ran and ran. By night he was far away. He must have found a herd of wild horses. For hunters sometimes tell about seeing a herd of wild horses in the mountains. In this herd of wild horses is a beautiful bay horse with four black legs and a coal black mane and a coal black tail.

No man will ever ride upon the back of Coaly-Bay.

Tommy, the Rosinback

Have you ever gone to the circus and seen a beautiful lady in white, dancing on the back of a horse? You may have seen Tommy.

Tommy was a beautiful white horse. He knew just what to do so that the lady that danced on his back would not fall off.

In the circus, Tommy is called a "rosinback." A "rosinback" is a horse on which men and beautiful ladies in the circus do "stunts." A "rosinback" must be a light colored horse because rosin is put on his back. This rosin keeps the people doing the stunts from falling. And this rosin does not show on the back of a light colored horse.

A "rosinback" has to be very carefully trained. Each time the horse goes around the circus ring, he must take just as many steps as he took the last time. When a man is jumping on and off the horse's back, that horse must be just where that man wants him to be.

A "rosinback," when he is in the ring, must not change his steps, whatever goes on around him. The horse must keep going around and around the circus ring in just the same way.

There once was a big wind that blew the circus tent away. A "rosinback" was in the circus ring going around and around. When the tent blew away, the "rosinback" kept going around and around the ring just as if nothing had happened.

When Tommy first came to the circus, you would have thought that he could never be trained to be a "rosinback." Tommy did not like men, and he would not let anybody ride on his back.

Mr. Branda had bought Tommy out West because Tommy was such a beautiful horse. No one told Mr. Branda that Tommy was a wild horse and would not let anyone ride him.

Tommy would not even let Mr. Branda touch him.

Mr. Branda's wife, Ella, was watching Tommy. She was the beautiful lady in white that danced on the back of a horse in the circus ring. She loved horses. She had always trained her own "rosinbacks."

"That horse is afraid of men," said Ella. "I know that some men have been very bad to him. Let me see if I can make friends with him."

"I am afraid that Tommy is a bad horse," said Mr. Branda, "I am afraid that he might hurt you."

Ella got a lump of sugar.

"You go away where Tommy cannot see you," said Ella. "I am going to make friends with Tommy."

Mr. Branda went behind a circus tent. But he watched to see that Ella was not hurt by the horse.

Very, very slowly, Ella went

closer to Tommy. All the time she kept talking to him.

"Come on, Tommy," said Ella. "I am not going to hurt you. I have something that you will like to eat. Come on, Tommy, I am your friend. I will not hurt you."

Tommy put up his ears. He seemed to like this soft voice. He liked to have this lady talk to him. He let the lady come close to him. He did not run away. The lady did not try to touch him. She held out her hand. And in her hand was something that Tommy wanted to eat.

That first time, it took a long

time before Tommy would eat
the lump of sugar out of Ella's
hand. All the time, Ella talked
to the horse in her soft voice.
And not once did she make the
horse afraid by trying to touch
him.

The next morning, Tommy
took something to eat from Ella's
hand. But this time, Tommy put
his soft nose up to Ella as if to
thank her. But when Ella put up
her other hand to touch Tommy
on the head, Tommy became
afraid and ran away.

"All right," said Ella. "You do
not want to be a friend with me.

I am going away and I am not going to bring you any more lumps of sugar."

Ella turned her back on Tommy and did not look at him. She did not talk to him in her soft voice. She just stood very still with her back to the horse.

Pretty soon, Tommy came to her. He put his head around to see if she had a lump of sugar in her hand, but she did not stay and talk to him.

"Goodbye, Tommy," said Ella. "I am going away."

Ella walked out of the yard and she did not look back.

Tommy went to the fence and looked after Ella. He wanted Ella to come back.

The next morning, Ella fed Tommy. The big horse let her brush him. He put his head down so that she could pat him.

Ella fed Tommy every morning. Then one morning she came with a saddle.

Ella talked to Tommy about the saddle. She showed him the saddle and let him smell it. At last, Tommy let Ella put the saddle on his back. And he let Ella get up in the saddle and ride him around the yard. He held his head high. And he put his feet down carefully as if he were trying not to hurt his lady.

From that time on, Tommy would do anything that Ella asked him to do. It was not long before Tommy became her "rosin-back" in the circus ring. She danced upon his back. And Tommy was always very careful not to do anything that might hurt his lady.

One time, Buffalo Bill wanted to buy Tommy because he wanted such a beautiful horse. He would have given Ella as much money as she asked for Tommy.

But Ella said,

"I could not sell Tommy. You just cannot sell one of your friends and Tommy and I are friends."

Mother Goose

Most horses do not like elephants. They are very much afraid of those great big animals.

But in a circus, all kinds of animals are together. They have to get used to one another.

Now Mother Goose was an old horse. She liked the elephants. And the elephants liked Mother Goose.

The man who looked after the elephants rode on Mother Goose. And wherever Mother Goose went, the elephants would follow.

One time, the elephants of the

circus ran away. They broke down fences and pulled up small trees. All the people were afraid of the elephants because they were so big.

The man who looked after the elephants got on Mother Goose. He rode out into the country. When the elephants saw Mother Goose, they did not want to run away. They liked Mother Goose.

Pretty soon the man rode back to the circus. All of the elephants were following Mother Goose. Each elephant went to its place in the elephant tent. And the men chained them to their places.

Mother Goose was getting very old. She got very tired walking ahead of the elephants in the Circus Parade. Mother Goose was put in the horse tent. She had a nice place to sleep. She had all she wanted to eat. She did not have to work any more taking care of the elephants.

But Mother Goose was not happy. And the elephants were not happy.

Every night, one of the big elephants would pull up his chain. He would go over to the horse tent. He wanted to see Mother Goose. The elephants even tried to get into the horse tent and sleep beside Mother Goose. Sometimes two or three elephants would go over to the horse tent and try to sleep with Mother Goose.

The other horses in the horse tent did not like the elephants. And the elephants did not like the other horses. Such a noise at night you never heard.

There was only one thing to do. And that was to let Mother Goose sleep in the elephant tent.

And that is why you would see an old horse sleeping in the elephant tent. The horse was too old to do any work. But she kept the elephants happy.

The man who looks after the elephants always says,

"A happy elephant is a good elephant."

Tony, Who Thought
for Himself

Tony was a beautiful Palomino horse. And Tony was a circus horse.

One day, a man named Derrick was sitting beside a road in the country. He was talking to a friend. The two men, who both loved horses, were talking about the right way to train a horse. Derrick had trained many circus horses.

"You watch what the horse does," said Derrick. "Many horses

shake their heads up and down when flies are around them. I give a horse a lump of sugar when he shakes his head up and down. Soon he knows that I want him to shake his head up and down. Each time, I hold my hand in the same way. Pretty soon when I hold my hand in this way, the horse will shake his head up and down. Then I can ask the horse whatever I want to. He will shake his head up and down. And people will think that he is saying 'yes'."

Just then the two men heard a

horse coming down the road. It was a beautiful golden horse, with long white tail. Derrick knew at once he must have that horse.

The man who was driving Tony was willing to sell him to Derrick right away. And Derrick took Tony to the circus.

Derrick thought he had got a very beautiful horse for his circus. But when he started to train Tony, he found that Tony was the smartest horse that he had ever tried to train.

Most circus horses do their

tricks in the same way every time they go into the circus ring. But Tony could think for himself. He would change his tricks when he wanted to.

Tony learned a trick from Derrick that always made the children laugh. Derrick would say to Tony,

"Funnyface, why don't you do what I tell you to do?"

Tony would act as if he was very angry at being called "Funnyface." He would run Derrick all around the circus ring. Then Derrick would call out to Tony,

"Beautiful, Beautiful, you are not a funnyface."

Then Tony would come and put his nose up to Derrick and would seem to talk in his ear.

At the end of the act, Tony would run Derrick out of the circus ring. And Derrick had to run fast or Tony would catch him. Then Tony would come back all by himself and bow to the people.

Tony loved the circus. He liked to do his tricks. But there was one thing that Tony did not like to do. Tony did not like to work in the way other horses do.

One day the friend of Derrick

had a little wagon that he had left at a farm house. He wanted to go and get it. But he needed a horse to pull the wagon.

Derrick said to his friend,

"Take Tony. Ride him to the farm house. He can pull your wagon back to the circus. It will do Tony good to get out into the country."

So the friend put a saddle on Tony and rode him out into the country to the farm house. He took the saddle off of Tony and put it into the wagon. Then he hitched Tony to the wagon. But

Tony would not pull the wagon. He just stood still.

The friend knew that Tony was so smart that he would not do what he did not want to do. So the friend left Tony at the farm and took the train back to the circus. He got another horse and rode him out to the farm.

He hitched this other horse to the wagon. Then he tied Tony to the back of the wagon and started out for the circus. But Tony bit the rope that he was tied with. He did not want to be tied to a wagon.

The man saw what he must do. So he started back to the circus in the wagon. Tony followed along behind. When he wanted to, he stopped and ate the green grass beside the road. Then he would catch up with the wagon again. He would not run away. He knew he was to go with the wagon. But he was not going to be tied to the wagon.

The man and the wagon and the other horse got back to the circus. And Tony, who thought for himself, had had a good time in the country. Tony would work hard doing his tricks. But he would not work like other horses and pull a wagon.

The White Horse Patrol

There are fifty beautiful white horses in the White Horse Patrol. And King was the white horse that would lead them in the parade.

King loved the parade. He loved the music. He held his head high. And he lifted his feet high as he kept time to the music. He loved to lead the White Horse Patrol.

The White Horse Patrol is made up of men called Shriners.

Each man owns a beautiful white horse. Every man has his own work, but part of the time these men ride and train their white horses. They teach them to go by twos, by fours, and by eights. They even teach some of the horses circus tricks.

For the White Horse Patrol is sometimes part of the Shriners Circus. The Shriners Circus plays in many cities. It makes money to help children who are sick.

Two of the horses, Silver Lady and Patsy, have learned to see-saw. How the children laugh to see two big white horses on a see-saw. Silver Lady goes up and Patsy goes down. Then up goes Patsy and down goes Silver Lady. If you watch very carefully you will see that Silver Lady goes up when she lifts her right front leg. Then Patsy lifts her right front leg and up she goes.

King, the beautiful horse who leads the parade, does the best act of the Shriners Circus. And this is the way it happened.

One day King was leading the parade down the street. He was very happy. The children along the street were calling out to him. And the music was playing.

King was feeling so happy that he stood on his back legs. He began to walk along with his front legs up high.

The children cried out,

"Look, look. The white horse is walking on his back legs. He is keeping time to the music with his front legs."

And now at the Shriners Circus, King walks all around the ring on his back legs. His front legs are up high. And it looks as if the beautiful horse is keeping time to the music.

No one had to teach King to do this trick. For this is a trick that King did all by himself, and when he saw how happy it made the children, he just went on doing it.

The Circus Fire

Tony thought Skippy was the bravest horse he had ever heard of. Tony was a policeman. He rode Skippy up and down the streets of a big city. One day Skippy showed Tony what a brave horse he was.

One morning Tony was riding Skippy down the street. Skippy threw up his head. Then Tony smelled smoke. He heard the fire trucks coming down the street. He and Skippy went after the fire trucks.

Now there are two things that

horses are very much afraid of. They are afraid of fire. And they are afraid of elephants.

As Tony and Skippy were going to the fire the street became full of people.

"The circus is on fire," cried the people. "The circus is on fire."

And then Skippy saw ten big elephants. They were coming right at him.

"Skippy, you are all right," said Tony. "The elephants will not hurt you." Skippy began to shake all over but he did not run away.

The elephant keeper was taking the elephants away from the fire. They went by Skippy, almost touching him. Each elephant held the tail of the elephant in front. Some of the elephants had been burned by the fire. But the elephants had done just what the keeper wanted them to do. And they were saved from the fire.

"Good boy, Skippy," said Tony. "You did not run away from the elephants. Let us get to the fire. Maybe we can help."

The tents of the circus were burning. There were animals and people running all about. Tony was glad that the show had not started. Fathers and mothers and children were not there.

Tony and Skippy rode to the tent where the horses were kept. The tent was full of smoke. The horses were very much afraid. They were running around and around in the tent. They would not do what their keepers wanted them to do.

The tent was beginning to burn. The keepers must get the horses out of the tent or they would all be burned.

"We must help get the horses out of the tent, Skippy. Go in, boy," said Tony. "Go into the tent."

Skippy was afraid of the fire. He was shaking all over.

"Go in, Skippy," said Tony. "Go into the tent." And Skippy went into the burning tent. A man called to Tony,

"Get the white horse. The white horse leads the parade. Get the white horse to go out of the tent. Then the other horses may follow the white horse."

"Skippy," said Tony, "get the white horse. Get the white horse."

The white horse was running around and around with the

other horses. The horses were kicking and biting. Some horses' manes and tails were burning. The horses were so afraid they did not know what they were doing.

The tent was getting so full of smoke that Tony and Skippy could hardly see.

Tony rode Skippy in among the kicking and biting horses. He could just see the white horse.

At last Tony got the rope that was on the head of the white horse. He pulled and pulled. Skippy started to lead the white horse out of the door of the tent.

And the other horses in the burning tent followed the white horse out of the tent.

The people who were watching saw a very funny circus parade. A policeman on a brown horse was pulling a white horse that was badly frightened. And behind the white horse came many badly frightened circus horses. Their manes and tails were burned but they were following the white horse, just as they did in the circus parade.

Old Dobbin

Dobbin was an old farm horse. He lived on a farm all his life. He always worked hard.

Dobbin was well cared for. He had all he wanted to eat. He had a nice place in the barn to sleep.

All the children on the farm loved old Dobbin. They sometimes would bring the old horse an apple, for he loved to eat apples.

Father sometimes let the children ride on Old Dobbin's back. Old Dobbin walked very carefully so that the children would not fall off. Father even let Baby Peter, who was only two years old, sit on Old Dobbin's back. But Father held Baby Peter so that he would not fall off.

One day Father had come back to the farm driving Old Dobbin. He drove into the carriage house and stopped so that the carriage would stay there. He took Old Dobbin from the carriage so that he could go to his place in the barn.

Dobbin went out of the carriage house and started for the

barn. Then Father saw something that made him very much afraid.

There, right in the barn doorway was Baby Peter. Father did not know the baby was anywhere around. Old Dobbin would walk right over Baby Peter as he went into the barn. And Old Dobbin had iron shoes on his feet that might hit Baby Peter and hurt him very much.

Father started to call out to Old Dobbin to stop him, but there was no time. Old Dobbin had just got to the barn doorway and to Baby Peter. But Old Dobbin knew that Baby Peter was there. Then the horse did something that showed how smart he was.

Old Dobbin stepped carefully over Baby Peter. And as he did this, he lifted one foot after the other very high. He did not want to hit Baby Peter with his feet. Baby Peter was sitting up. But the horse lifted each foot so high that Baby Peter was not hurt at all.

Father ran and picked up Baby Peter. Then he and Baby Peter went into the barn and talked to Old Dobbin. Father was so glad

Old Dobbin was such a good old horse. He was glad that Old Dobbin loved the children. Father gave Old Dobbin some oats to eat and he gave Old Dobbin an apple too.

Dan

Dan was a farm horse, and he liked to eat oats. Every night Jim gave Dan a good supper. Jim liked Dan, for he was a good horse and worked hard.

Every night, Jim closed the barn door and put a bar across on the inside. Then he went out the little door of the barn.

One day, when Jim went out to the barn in the morning, the big barn door was open. Jim thought that Dan might be gone. But Dan was there in his place. Whoever had opened the barn door had not hurt Dan.

That night, Jim was very careful to see that the barn door was closed with the bar across the door on the inside. But in the morning, the door was open and the bar was on the ground. Dan was in his place.

Jim could not understand it. Day after day, the door was closed with the bar at night and in the morning it would be open, with the bar on the ground.

One day the man who lived on the next farm came to Jim's father. The man said,

"Do you know that your horse, Dan, comes over to my farm in the night time and eats my oats?"

Jim and his father could not understand how Dan could be in the barn each morning but be in the farmer's oats every night. Who opened the barn door?

"I am going to sleep in the barn," said Jim to his father. "I am going to find out who is opening the barn door."

Jim went to sleep in the barn. In the night there was a noise. Jim turned his flashlight on the barn door.

There was Dan lifting the bar from the barn door with his teeth.

So that was how it happened. In the night, Dan had opened the door, gone to the other farm and eaten the oats.

When Jim told his father who it was that opened the barn door, they both laughed.

"Dan is a smart horse," said Jim's father. "But he must not go and eat the farmer's oats."

"I will fix that barn door so that Dan cannot open it," said Jim.

Jim and his father put a big

bar on the outside of the barn door. At night, Jim would close the barn door and on the outside he would put this big bar across the door. Dan could not lift it because he could not get to it.

For three nights, the barn door stayed closed. But one morning Jim found the barn door open. The bar on the outside had been broken.

"I am going to sleep in the barn again," said Jim. "I am going to find out how that barn door was opened."

Again Jim went to sleep in the

barn. In the night he heard a big noise. Jim turned his flashlight on the barn door.

There was Dan with his back to the door. He was pushing and pushing on the door. The bar on the outside of the door broke. And the door opened. Jim called to Dan and put him back in his place in the barn. Dan did not get to the oats that night.

Jim's father knew that he had to fix that door so that Dan could not get out. He got a long iron bar. He fixed the iron bar across the door on the outside.

At night, Jim gave Dan a good

supper. Then when he went out he closed the barn door and put the iron bar across it.

Dan tried to push the door out, but the iron bar was too strong. The barn door was not opened. And Dan did not get to eat the farmer's oats.

The Old White Horse

Charley was just an old white horse. But Charley was happy because he had work to do. He worked at a factory.

Every day Mr. Dooley took the old white horse to the yard of the factory. In the yard stood a big pole with a big wheel on the top of it. Mr. Dooley hitched Charley to a smaller pole that turned the big pole. As the big pole turned, the wheel at the top went round and round.

All day long Charley walked

around and around the big pole. As he walked around, he pulled the small pole that turned the big pole that turned the big wheel. And the big wheel was fixed so that it turned some wheels in the factory.

All year long, Charley walked around and around in the factory yard. In the rain and in the sun, Charley worked every day. And Charley liked his work.

When the factory whistle blew in the morning, the men started to work in the factory. And Charley started to work in the factory yard. When the factory whistle blew again, the men in the factory stopped to eat. And Mr. Dooley brought Charley something to eat too.

When the factory whistle blew for men to stop their work for the day, Charley stopped his work. Mr. Dooley took the old white horse back home. Charley was very happy with his work at the factory.

But one day Mr. Dooley got a young black horse. He hitched the black horse to a wagon. He tied Charley to the back of the wagon. Charley did not know what was going to happen.

Mr. Dooley got into the wagon. He did not go to the factory yard. He went out into the country where the grass was green. At last he stopped and took Charley from the back of the wagon. He opened a gate and put Charley into a green pasture.

Charley went into the pasture and stood there. He did not know what to do.

"Charley, my boy," said Mr. Dooley, "you are going to have a fine time. All day long you can eat the green grass. You will not have to work any more. And I will come to see you and bring you a red apple."

Mr. Dooley got into the wagon and went back to the factory.

For a long time Charley stood just where Mr. Dooley had left him. Charley was not happy. Every now and then he lifted his head. He wanted to hear the noise of the factory.

After a time Charley ate some green grass and found it very good. When the sun got hot the old horse went and stood under a tree that was in the pasture.

The grass was very good and

the sun was warm. But Charley, the old white horse, was not happy. He had no work to do. Very soon he did not even want to eat the green grass. The old horse began to look tired and sick.

Then one day the wind blew from the factory to the pasture. Charley's head went up. He heard the factory whistle. Charley walked right to the tree that was in the pasture. He began to walk around and around the tree just as he had walked around and around the big pole in the factory yard.

All morning Charley walked around the tree. The old white horse was very happy. When he heard the whistle again, Charley stopped walking around the tree. He ate some of the grass in the pasture. He went down to the little river and had a drink of water. Everything was so good, for Charley had worked all morning.

Very softly he heard the whistle that called the men at the factory back to work. Charley went right back to the tree that was in the pasture. He walked around and around the tree. He did not stop until he heard the whistle that told the men at the factory it was time to go home.

Then Charley ran and jumped about. He played in the pasture just like a young horse. And when he was tired of running and jumping he ate the green grass and went to sleep.

Now Charley knew what to do. Even when the wind did not blow from the factory, Charley went to work. Every morning he walked around and around the tree in the pasture. And after he had stopped to eat, he again walked around and around the tree in the pasture.

Charley, the old white horse, was happy. Every day he had his work to do.

O'Mally's Horse

Jason was a poor old horse that saved the lives of more children in New York City than any horse that ever lived.

One day a man and his daughter brought an old horse to the Animal Hospital. The old horse was Jason. One foot hurt the horse so badly that he could not walk upon it.

The man wanted to find out if the old horse could get well. The old horse pulled the man's wagon.

If the horse could not pull the coal wagon, the horse would be killed.

The girl loved the horse. She did not want the old horse killed.

The doctor and O'Mally, a young man who was going to become a doctor, looked at the horse's foot very carefully. Then the doctor said that the old horse would never be well again. He could not pull the coal wagon.

The girl began to cry. She knew her father would sell the horse to have it killed.

The father took the old horse away. But the girl did not go

with him. She stayed at the
Animal Hospital. She wanted to
talk to O'Mally, the young man
who wanted to become an animal
doctor.

"You are a doctor of horses,"
said the girl. "Please do something for Jason. I love Jason and
I do not want him killed."

"I am not a doctor of horses
now," said O'Mally. "But some
day I will be."

"You could talk to the doctor
of the Animal Hospital and get
him to do something for Jason,"
said the girl.

O'Mally talked to the doctor

again. But the doctor said that nothing could be done to help the foot of the old horse.

When O'Mally told the girl what the doctor had said, she began to cry again. Then O'Mally said,

"Your father will get only five dollars for the horse when he sells him. I have saved seven dollars. I will buy Jason for seven dollars."

The girl took the money and thanked the young man very much. Then she ran home to get Jason. And O'Mally for the first time in his life owned a horse.

Jason came to live at the Animal Hospital. Jason was not sick. He was old and he had a hurt foot. He could not pull a wagon. But he could help the doctors at the Animal Hospital. O'Mally was going to use Jason for some work that was being done with horses.

All the time doctors are trying to find out how to help sick people and keep them well. Some of the doctors in New York City were trying to find a cure for the bad sickness called diphtheria. Every year diphtheria killed many children.

The doctors would make little animals sick with diphtheria. Then they would try to find something to give the little animals to make them well. At last the doctors had found out that if they made a horse just a little sick with diphtheria, the horse's blood would make something called antitoxin and the horse would get well.

The doctor would take some blood from this horse and from this blood take the part that had the antitoxin in it. They would give this antitoxin to the little animals that were sick with diphtheria. And the sick animals got well.

Now, doctors in New York City wanted to give children who were sick with diphtheria some of the blood of a horse who had made antitoxin. And so in the Animal Hospital there were many horses who had been made just a little sick with diphtheria. These horses were making antitoxin in their blood.

Jason, the old horse with the hurt foot, was given a nice clean place to live. He ate all that he wanted. People were kind to him.

And O'Mally and the girl who loved him came every day to see him. Jason was a very happy horse.

Jason was made a little sick with diphtheria. Then Jason began to make antitoxin in his blood for the children of New York City.

The doctors found that the antitoxin from the blood of Jason was the best antitoxin that they had. They gave it to the children who were sick with diphtheria. And the sick children got well.

Jason lived many years at the Animal Hospital. Year after year he made antitoxin in his blood for the children of New York City. And that is how he saved the lives of more children in New York City than any horse that ever lived.

Carbine

Carbine was a fine race horse. And Carbine knew what he wanted. He wanted to win races.

Carbine was a good horse. But when Carbine did not win a race, he became very angry. He would jump about. He would kick and bite.

Sometimes a boy will get angry when he does not win a game. But a boy knows that he cannot win all the time. He just tries harder the next time he plays.

But Carbine thought that he could win every race. It was

funny to see him get so angry when he did not win. The boys who took care of Carbine would say to him,

"Carbine, you just try harder the next time. Then you will win the race."

Pretty soon Carbine would hang his head. It looked as if he knew he had been acting badly.

The boys that took care of the horses all loved Carbine. They laughed at his funny ways.

There was one thing that Carbine did not like. He did not like to get his ears wet. Carbine did not care if his back got wet.

He did not care if his legs got wet. But he would not get out in the rain and get his ears wet.

One day there was to be a great race. It started to rain just as it was time for the race. All the other horses were ready for the race. But Carbine would not go out into the rain.

The man who looked after Carbine did not know what to do. He was sure that Carbine could win the race. But Carbine did not like to get his ears wet. He would not go out into the rain.

The man got an umbrella. He

walked beside the horse holding the umbrella over the horse's head. This was the only way to get Carbine to go out into the rain.

Everybody laughed when they saw Carbine with the man holding the umbrella over the horse's head.

When Carbine got to the start of the race and saw the other horses, he forgot all about the rain. Carbine wanted to win. He forgot all about his ears. Carbine ran and won the race.

The man who looked after Carbine made him a little umbrella. The little umbrella was fixed over Carbine's head. It just covered his ears.

It was very funny to see this beautiful race horse on a rainy day. Oh, how fast he could run with his little umbrella keeping his ears from getting wet.

Black Gold

U-see-it was a horse owned by
Al Hoots, an Indian who lived on
a farm in Oklahoma. U-see-it had
a little black colt. And Al Hoots
named the little black colt Black
Gold. For oil had been found on
the farm of Al Hoots, and in
Oklahoma, oil is called Black
Gold.

U-see-it had won some races.
And Al Hoots was sure that her
little colt, Black Gold, was going
to grow up to be a fine race
horse.

Black Gold was trained by an

old Indian named Webb, who had trained U-see-it. Webb lived with the colt, Black Gold. He talked to the colt. And Black Gold seemed to understand what Webb told him.

Al Hoots got very sick. He knew he was going to die. He said to his wife, Rosa,

"Never, never sell Black Gold. He is going to grow up to be a fine race horse. Some day he will win the big race." The "big race" was the Kentucky Derby.

The oil that had been found on Al Hoots' farm made Rosa very rich. She had money to take

Black Gold and his trainer, Webb, to any race in the country.

Black Gold began to win. Everyone began to talk about the black horse that was owned by Rosa. He was a fine race horse.

And then came the big race, the Kentucky Derby.

Before Al Hoots had died, Rosa had told him she would look after Black Gold. Some day she would take Black Gold to the big race. And now the day had come.

Webb, in an old raincoat that he always had on, was with Black Gold.

"Now, my baby," said Webb

into Black Gold's ear. "This is the big day. Your mother was a good race horse. But you are a better race horse than your mother. Al Hoots said before he died that you would win the big race. Now this is the day. You just have to win."

Black Gold looked as if he knew what Webb was saying to him.

Rosa Hoots was in a box at the Kentucky Derby. No one knew what she was thinking. She was thinking of what Al Hoots had said to her before he died, "Some day Black Gold will win the big race."

The horses were ready for the race. Some of the horses were jumping around. But Black Gold was very good. He liked the man who was riding him. He did just what he was told to do.

At last the horses were off.

But Black Gold was not ahead. Two horses were ahead of him, and he could not get by them.

The horses were running very fast. It was a long race. Two horses were still ahead of Black Gold.

And now the horses were on the last of the race.

The boy on Black Gold talked

to Black Gold. Black Gold knew what the boy wanted him to do.

Black Gold ran around one horse. Now all the horses were running just as fast as they could run.

Only one horse was ahead of Black Gold. Black Gold ran right ahead of that horse.

Black Gold won the Kentucky Derby.

The old Indian, Webb, had watched the race without a smile. And Rosa Hoots had watched the race without a smile.

They were thinking of Al Hoots. How happy Al Hoots had been

when U-see-it had won races. And how happy Al Hoots would have been to know that U-see-it's black colt had won the Derby.

Black Gold held his head high when they put the red roses on him, as they always do on the winner of the Kentucky Derby.

The trainer, Webb, in his old raincoat, and Rosa Hoots stood beside the black horse and knew that Al Hoots would have been so happy to have been there.

But because they were Indians, no one could have told what they were thinking.

Prince Hal

Prince Hal was a beautiful horse. He had been trained to jump over high fences. He was the best jumper in England and France and America.

Prince Hal knew just what he wanted to do. But his owner, Pat Smythe, knew that a jumper must always do just what his rider tells him to do. So she had to be very careful how she trained Prince Hal. And she had to train him for a long time.

Every morning after breakfast, Prince Hal was brushed and made ready to go to jumping school. For Prince Hal had to learn many things before he became the best jumper in England.

In the morning, horses like to go for a run. They like to turn and jump just as their riders tell them to. But not Prince Hal. In the morning he did not want to do any of the things other horses wanted to do.

After breakfast, Prince Hal was sleepy. After he had been brushed to go out, the beautiful horse would lie down and go to sleep again. Then the boys who looked after the horses would have to brush him all over again.

When, at last, Prince Hal went out for his training in the morning, he could hardly walk. The other horses would be running about and having a good time. But Prince Hal just stood with his head down and his eyes almost closed. He looked so very, very tired. You would never think that this was the best jumper in England.

But when Prince Hal was at a Horse Show, he was not the same horse. He held his head up. He looked at everything about him.

He looked carefully at the fences he was going to jump over. He seemed to be making up his mind how high they were. And how beautiful Prince Hal looked as he jumped over those fences in the Horse Show. He jumped over higher fences than the other horses did and he jumped more beautifully.

But next morning, Prince Hal looked like a tired, sleepy horse. He did not look like a jumper at all.

Prince Hal was a tease. Sometimes he would tease Pat. After jumping all the fences at the

Horse Show and being the very best horse in the Show, he would try to throw Pat off his back. Pat was such a good rider that he could never throw her. But Prince Hal seemed to be saying,

"Look here, Pat. I jumped over all those fences just like you wanted me to. Now I am going to do just what I want to do."

When Prince Hal was at home, he would sometimes tease Pat. One day when she was patting him, he bit the buttons off her coat. Then he held the buttons in his mouth and looked as if he had never done anything at all.

One day, Prince Hal had to have new horse shoes put on. He stood very quietly beside the blacksmith. And the blacksmith worked hard putting on the new shoes.

Prince Hal must have thought that the blacksmith had something funny across his back. It was the blacksmith's suspenders. Prince Hal watched those suspenders.

When no one was looking, Prince Hal took those suspenders in his teeth and pulled them out as far as they would go. Then suddenly he let go.

The blacksmith jumped when the suspenders hit his back. But when he looked up, Prince Hal was looking the other way. Prince Hal looked as if he had never done anything at all.

Little Horses

At the Golden Gate Exposition, in San Francisco, there were three little horses. These horses were no bigger than dogs.

Two little boys were looking at the horses. One boy said to the other boy, "Those horses are not horses. They are just dogs that look like horses."

But the boy was not right. He was looking at three little horses.

This is how there came to be little horses.

There was an Indian named Smiley. He was a Supai Indian.

And his people lived in the Grand Canyon of Arizona.

One day Smiley was running away from some Indians who were trying to kill him. He had with him a father and a mother horse and a colt or baby horse.

It was hard for the horses to go over the rocks. Smiley thought that he had better hide the horses in a canyon. Then he could get to his people before the other Indians could catch him.

Smiley found a small canyon where there was green grass and water. He put the horses in this canyon. He was sure no Indians would ever find them. Then Smiley went on to his people.

Then the cold time came. The snow came down and covered the rocks. Smiley could not get back to the canyon. But he knew that the horses had grass to eat and water to drink.

When it was warm again, Smiley went back to the place where he had left the horses. But because of the snow, big rocks had fallen down the sides of the canyon. One could get into the canyon only if he went down a rope. And horses could get out of the canyon only if they were pulled up by ropes. The big rocks had closed the canyon.

Smiley was the only Indian that knew there were three horses in the canyon, a father horse and a mother horse and a colt or baby horse. And he could not get them out of the canyon.

Year after year, the horses stayed in the canyon. There was grass for them to eat. There was water for them to drink. And year after year there were baby colts.

And now something happened that no one thought of. The horses that lived in the canyon did not grow very big. Not much sun got down into the canyon. And it is the sun that makes things grow. There was not much grass in the canyon. And the grass did have in it all the things that make animals grow. Year after year, the colts were smaller and smaller. And when they were big they were not as big as their fathers and mothers.

And then Supai Smiley became Chief of his people. He took his people to see the little horses. He said to his people,

"The Great One has put the little horses into Little Horse Canyon. The Great One has given these little horses to the Supai Indians. My people must never tell anyone about the little horses that live in Little Horse Canyon."

Years went by, and the horses became smaller and smaller. What would you think of a colt that was no bigger than a rabbit? What would you think of a mother horse no bigger than a sheep?

Supai Smiley became an old man. And there was one white man that the Old Indian liked very much. This white man, named Jack Tooker, had been very good to Supai Smiley.

One day Chief Supai Smiley

took Jack to Little Horse Canyon. The old Indian let Jack see something that no white man had ever seen before. Jack Tooker saw the little horses.

Then Chief Supai Smiley told Jack about the three horses that he had left in the canyon. That had been when he was young and now Chief Supai Smiley was almost a hundred years old.

"When I die," said Chief Supai Smiley, "you may tell the white man about my little horses. But as long as I live, my friend, you are to be the only white man that is to know about the little horses."

"Chief Smiley," said Jack Tooker, "if I should tell the white man about your little horses, no one would believe that there could be a father horse no bigger than a dog. Or a colt no bigger than a rabbit."

"Yes," said the old Indian Chief. "The white men would not believe. They would have to see the little horses. When I am gone, my people will let you have three of the little horses to show to the white man."

Old Chief Supai Smiley was over a hundred years old when he died. It was then that Jack Tooker went to the Supai Indians. They helped him get three of the little horses out of Little Horse Canyon.

The three little horses were taken to the Golden Gate Exposition in San Francisco.

And this is how there came to be little horses in Little Horse Canyon. The Supai Indians still think that the Great One has given them the little horses to look after. No more horses are being taken out of Little Horse Canyon.

The Long, Long Walk

If you walk a mile, you may think that is a long walk. And if you should walk a hundred miles, you would think that was a very long walk.

Mancha was a South American horse. And he walked 10,000 miles. He walked up and down high mountains. He walked over rocks. He walked through great woods where there were many kinds of wild animals.

But the part of his long, long walk that Mancha did not like at all was when he walked down the streets of New York City. He did not like the hard streets. He did not like so many people. He did not like the noise that so many cars made.

Mancha and Gato and Mr. Tschiffely had started from Buenos Aires in South America. It took over two years for Mancha, Gato, and Mr. Tschiffely to get from Buenos Aires to New York City. And the long, long walk was 10,000 miles.

Mr. A. E. Tschiffely was a school teacher. Part of every year he went out with the cowboys of South America. The ponies he and the cowboys rode were small and very strong. Mr Tschiffely got to thinking that he would like to ride a South American cow pony from Buenos Aires to New York City.

A good friend who had many cow ponies gave Mr. Tschiffely Mancha and Gato. Mancha was a red and white horse. He had four white legs and a white face. He was very smart and very wild. He held his head high and looked at everything around him. Mancha would never let any one ride him but Mr. Tschiffely. When he found that he could not throw Mr.

Tschiffely off his back, he became a very good horse.

Gato was a wild horse too. But he was more quiet than Mancha. Gato made a good pack horse. He followed behind Mancha, for Mancha always wanted to go first.

One day Mr. Tschiffely was walking along a little mountain road. Mancha was behind him, and then came Gato. Suddenly Gato went over the side of the mountain. He would surely have been killed if a tree on the side of the mountain had not stopped his fall. Some Indians came by and helped Mr. Tschiffely get Gato up the side of the mountain. Ropes were tied to Gato. The Indians pulled and pulled. At last Gato was on the road again.

At another time, an Indian had to take Mr. Tschiffely and the two horses over a rope bridge. The rope bridge was over a river up in the mountains. There was no other way to get across the river. The bridge was four feet from side to side and four hundred feet long. Even a man would be afraid to walk across such a bridge. Mr. Tschiffely did not know how he was going to get two horses across the bridge.

The Indian walked first with a rope to Mancha's head. Mr. Tschiffely held Mancha's tail and talked to him all the time that he was walking across the bridge. Once the horse stopped when the bridge began to shake. If the horse had tried to turn around he would have fallen off the bridge. But Mancha heard his Master talking to him. When the bridge stopped shaking, he went on. Mancha and the Indian and Mr.

Tschiffely got across the bridge at last.

Then the Indian and Mr. Tschiffely had to go back across the bridge and lead Gato across. Gato was a quiet horse and went very carefully across the bridge.

Another time Mancha and Gato had to swim across a river. It had rained and rained. The river was very full of water. Mr. Tschiffely had to find an Indian whose work was to help animals swim across the river. Many times he would take cows across the river.

Many people came to watch

the horses swim across the river. It was going to be a very hard swim, for the river was so full of water. Some people thought that the horses could not get across. Other people said that the Indian would get the horses across, for he knew the river.

The Indian looked at the river very carefully. And then he took the horses into the water. Mancha and Gato were good swimmers. But the water carried them down the river. It seemed a very long time to Mr. Tschiffely. But at last he heard a noise from the people on the other side of the river. He knew that his horses were across the river.

The Indians would not let Mr. Tschiffely swim across the river for he did not know the bad places in the river. He had to go across the river in a big basket hanging on a rope. The basket was pulled across the river by the people.

Something very funny happened one day. The horses were going through the deep woods. Many bugs were biting the horses. The horses tried to keep the bugs off with their tails. Mr. Tschiffely wanted to help them.

Mr. Tschiffely killed some of

the birds so as to get something to eat. The birds had many colored feathers. Mr. Tschiffely took some of these feathers and tied them to the horses' tails to help them keep off the bugs.

Mancha looked back to see what Mr. Tschiffely was doing. He saw the colored feathers on the end of his tail. He was so afraid that he ran away.

Gato saw the feathers on his tail too. He ran away after Mancha. Mr. Tschiffely had a hard time getting his two horses back again. He never tried to tie feathers to their tails again.

At last Mr. Tschiffely and the two horses got to the United States. Mancha and Gato did not like the hard roads. When they could, they walked on the grass beside the road.

There were too many cars. And they went so fast. One car ran into Mancha and hurt him. It was a good thing that the car did not kill the little horse that had walked so far.

Mr. Tschiffely was afraid that if he had two horses on the road, one of them would be hit. So he left Gato at St. Louis. Then Gato went to New York by train. Mr.

Tschiffely did not need a pack horse to carry all his things. Now he could always find a place to eat and a place to sleep.

Mr. Tschiffely rode Mancha all the way to New York City. And that was the end of the 10,000 miles long long ride.

Mr. Tschiffely told people about his long long ride. He told them about his two strong brave horses. And when he got back to South Ameria he wrote a book about his 10,000 mile ride.

But the two brave horses did not stay in New York. And they did not walk back to Buenos

Aires. Mr. Tschiffely took the two horses with him on a ship.

When the ship got to Buenos Aires, Mr. Tschiffely took Mancha and Gato back to the place which was their home. They were put in a pasture, where they could run and where they could eat as much of the grass as they wanted to. Their work was done.